SAYING THE WORLD

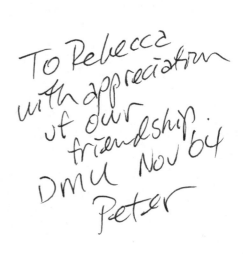

To Rebecca
with appreciation
of our
friendship.
DMU Nov '04
Peter

2002 HAYDEN CARRUTH AWARD

The Hayden Carruth Award was established in 1998 to honor the most distinguished first, second, or third book manuscript from nearly one thousand entries received at Copper Canyon Press.

PREVIOUS WINNERS

1999 Sascha Feinstein, *Misterioso*
2000 Rebecca Wee, *Uncertain Grace*
2001 Jenny Factor, *Unraveling at the Name*

SAYING THE WORLD

PETER PEREIRA

COPPER CANYON PRESS

Copper Canyon Press is in residence under the auspices of the Centrum
Foundation at Fort Worden State Park in Port Townsend, Washington.
Centrum sponsors artist residencies, education workshops for Washington
State students and teachers, Blues, Jazz, and Fiddle Tunes festivals, classical
music performances, and the Port Townsend Writers' Conference.

LIBRARY OF CONGRESS CATALOGING-IN-PUBLICATION DATA

Pereira, Peter, 1959–
  Saying the world / Peter Pereira.— 1st ed.
     p. cm.
  ISBN 1-55659-197-7 (pbk. : alk. paper)
  1. Physicians—Poetry. 2. Medicine—Poetry. I. Title.
  PS3616.E74S29 2003
  811'.6--dc21

                                          2003008475

FIRST EDITION
98765432
FIRST PRINTING

COPPER CANYON PRESS
Post Office Box 271
Port Townsend, Washington 98368
www.coppercanyonpress.org

FOR DEAN ALLAN

ACKNOWLEDGMENTS

Special thanks to Greg Orr and Sam Hamill for choosing my manuscript; to Mary Jane Knecht, Michael Wiegers, and all of the staff at Copper Canyon Press—you are amazing. Thanks also to several writers who influenced the development of these poems: Sharon Bryan, Jeff Crandall, T. Clear, Linda Greenmun, Margaret Hodge, Kathryn Hunt, Ted McMahon, and Gary Winans.

Grateful acknowledgment is made to the following magazines and anthologies, where versions of these poems first appeared.

Arnazella
Bellowing Ark
Crab Creek Review
Evergreen Chronicles
Jack Straw Writers
Journal of the American Medical Association
King County Arts Commission: Poetry on the Buses
LitRag
Manzanita Quarterly
Mudfish
The Nation
North Dakota Quarterly
Northwest Gay and Lesbian Reader
Poetry East
PoetsWest
The Raven Chronicles
Santa Clara Review
Seattle Review
Signals
Slipstream #14: Sex, Food, Death
Spindrift
Switched-on Gutenberg

Gents, Bad Boys, and Barbarians: New Gay Male Poetry (ed. Rudy Kikel, Alyson Publications, 1994)

To Come to Light: Perspectives on Chronic Illness in Modern Literature (ed. Amy Bonomi, Whit Press, 2002)

Uncharted Lines: Poems from the Journal of the American Medical Association (ed. Charlene Breedlove, Boaz Publishing Company, 1998)

Some of these poems also appeared in a limited edition fine letterpress chapbook, *The Lost Twin,* produced by Grey Spider Press with the support of the King County Arts Commission.

Finally, I would like to thank Artist Trust, the Seattle Arts Commission, and the Jack Straw Writers Program for poetry fellowships that encouraged the completion of this manuscript.

CONTENTS

III

SAYING THE WORLD

NOSOPHILIA

—love of affliction

For one it's insomnia, tremor, migraine.
Another has hangnails, hives, boils.
Airsick. Seasick. Incontinent. Fat.
Such misery loves company: a listening ear.

How else count, recount what woes?
Pimples that burn. Fevers that shiver.
Shinsplint. Bowleg. Backache. Rupture.
What pains us makes us *us*.

Flatus. Halitosis. Heartburn. Hiccup.
Color-blind. Cross-eyed. Piles. Palsy.
What makes us *absolutely*.
Bunion. Harelip. Warts and all.

I

FETUS PAPYRACEOUS

Sometimes one of the twins dies
in utero, without his mother
ever knowing she'd been twice blessed.
Hungry for life, the living twin
will absorb his double and, growing,
compress him until all that's left
is a tiny shape made flat, a silhouette
of the life it once contained.
While the one child is born pink
and howling into his parents' arms,
the other remains a faint imprint
barely visible in the translucent web
of amniotic membranes—a fetal hieroglyph.
Some people believe twins have
only one soul between them.
If that's true, how many
of us are born half—
ignorant of our paper twin, the ghostly
shroud of an other self,
the blank page onto which all
our imagined lives are written.

INTERN

Always the ritual of morning rounds: huddled
outside a new admit's door—clipboards, white coats,
scrubs, beepers—the lucky ones showered
and perhaps a few hours' sleep, a medical student
stumbling through case presentation, the ward attending
flicking her perfect nails. We'd try not to remember
how none of us had time to pee or to eat,
as we nattered endlessly the minutiae of Fluid Management.

From room to room we wound our way
past meal trays, tray tables, carts of syringes;
past stacks of needles, gauzes, tape, liters of intravenous
piled like sandbags; past hissing tanks of oxygen,
paper cups of pills gathered at the bedside,
commodes on rollers; the bedlam
of medical floors packed to the rafters with patients,
visiting families, and the potted flowers they scatter behind them.

To the manic quiet of Intensive Care,
stroke-numbed or sedated bodies
afloat on air mattresses, the huff and swish of ventilators,
the Teenage Homecoming Car Crash Victim
suspended in halo traction,
both eyes wide open and gooped with Vaseline,
mindless as we tote his Ins and Outs amid
burnt smell of ulcer blood, putrid chest tube drainage,
his meager urine dark as coffee.

I remember telemetry monitors pinging and dinging,
the overhead of a code being called,
cardiac surgeons cracking open the chest
of a post-op as if it were a Christmas turkey,
injecting the epinephrine needle directly into the heart.
I remember O_2 sats and blood pressures bottoming out,
eyes rolling back and the sickly ashen color
of a face before death.

At best it was *Star Trek: The Next Generation,*
our team marching the pristine halls of a great
Medical Center in the Sky, no disease immune
to the perfect rays of our healing weapons.
At worst it was Dante's *Inferno,* stuttering fluorescents
dimly lighting each unhealed foot ulcer
and abdominal wound dehiscence,
as we worked without rest for days on end,
sometimes never stopping to see the sun.

I remember one June morning the last week of call,
a woman who'd been laboring all night
panting and screaming and begging for us
to *take the baby now,*
oxygen mask strapped to her face
like a plane passenger in a nosedive,
fetal monitor in a brady, her legs wide open,
my hands shaking as I placed the forceps
on the vernix-smeared vertex and pulled...
and pulled... and pulled...

FIRST CRASH CESAREAN

Hold it like a wand, you say
as I guide the blade across shaved skin,
into layers of yellow fat and fascia
stained crimson. With gloved fingers
we tug at the wound's gaping edges
until we've exposed the bulging uterus,
round and smooth as a giant d'Anjou pear.
Only minutes ago, I wrote the words *fetal distress*
and panting she signed consent to open her belly.
Now her baby is like Houdini
jacketed inside a treasure chest five fathoms
down, mouth gagged, lungs bursting, time running out.
You palpate the rotation and lie, then show
me the spot in the thin lower segment
where you want me to begin; I trace
lightly with the gleaming scalpel
a gentle curve the shape of a smile.
Slower, you say, as the amniotic membranes
balloon through the lips, then rupture,
there's nothing between us and baby now.
You guide my blind hand into the meconium-stained
pool, and I am the first to touch her slumbering
fetus, enfolded like an unhatched gosling
in its taut shell of muscle and blood.
Now lift without bending your elbow,
you say, *then grab hold of an ankle.*
As I wonder what immutable law
of gravity such levitation would defy,
the preemie delivers easily by the breech, first
one tiny leg and then the other, then blue
body all grimace and fists, the coiling umbilical
cord wrapped tightly twice around his neck.
Wedging clamps and scissors under the noose,
you cut the babe free and its toothless mouth
gasps for its first true breath as Dad's flashbulb

bursts and the float nurse applauds, *It's a boy!*
Like a magic trick, you say quietly, smiling
behind your mask. Yes, I think,
placing the closing stitch in her uterus,
like pulling a rabbit out of a hat.

BABY MADE OF FLOWERS

Close to term, as poppies bloomed
and bluebirds hummed in the honeysuckle,
the baby began to nestle
its soft cranium into her pelvis's
narrow doorway, and she knew
the day was near. Until one morning,
pushing gently on a knee,
she felt the once squirming presence
grow strangely motionless and heavy.
An hour later the ultrasound wand
searched the silent depths of her womb
and the midwife said, "I'm sorry,
I can't find a heartbeat."

But even a baby who is dead must still be born.

Induced labor like a sickness—
each convulsing contraction full of grief,
an inconsolable wailing—she pushed
and pushed until the tiny body wrapped in pink
was handed to her, and its two blue feet
took their only steps across a sheet of paper.
Belly empty and shriveled,
breasts swollen with milk,
she is a bleeding woman with no baby
to feed, to comfort. Her empty house
slowly filling with flowers.

HYDROCEPHALIC

How to describe this light?
Globe held to malleable cranium, the glow
inside a quaver—candle-flame
suspended in molten glass.

Then the rhythmic flippering of sightless
eyes rolling back and back.

Mouth that will never form words
rooting for a breast that isn't there.

The Vietnamese grandparents say
he was born this way because his mother
acted without thinking—
their proof her daily absence.

What transpires inside this vault
where there can be no images, no thoughts?
Oceanic vibration. Whale song. Voice of angels.
Pure tone of an empty bell.

HER NAME IS ROSE

With a boil the size of an egg
protruding from her right hip,
she knows what I must do,
and to stall me has locked herself
inside the bathroom, bargaining
for a way out.

But it's too late: I've seen
the oozing wounds stopped up with bits
of toilet paper and tape, the scarified
pockets that crater the surface
of her arms, buttocks, thighs.

A mean fix torched her last vein
years ago, and she's been banging the dope
ever since, puncturing her body
like a juju doll. She wants to kick,
but not now.

I'm not gonna lie to you, she says
in a velvet voice. I already know what she's after:
something stronger than local, a few Percocet, a shot of Demerol
before she'll let me begin.

All I can tell you is, when the abscess finally drains
the odor is so foul it's evil.

And I'm not sure, driving home
later that night, still smelling the pallid citrus,
whether it's merely hallucination, the way
her memory inhabits me; or if being
in that same room, inhaling
that same air, made some of her
part of me.

                    And whose veins
are these, beginning to twitch?

MURMUR

They cut open his chest
and split the ribs, stitched
bits of leg veins
to the outside of his heart,
patched it all together
and stapled him shut,
sent him home.

Now he feels a turbulence
like a bird fluttering inside him.
As if his heart's old house
has a bad door that won't close,
shudders in the wind.

I place the cold, hard coin
of my stethoscope on his bare chest,
touching down on each of the four places,
medical school's rote lessons a thing of habit
as I listen for the *Tennessee*...
Tennessee... of a stiffened ventricle,
the *Kentucky*... *Kentucky*...
of congestive failure.

Systole, diastole... lub-
dub... lub-dub...,
I count ten healthy beats,
watch him breathe.

Perhaps it was the two hours on bypass,
the six weeks he missed work
for the first time in his life, or
how like an infant he needed others
to help him rise from a chair,
take his first steps around the unit.

I fold away my stethoscope.
He traces the pink zipper of a scar
down the front of his chest,
tells me he's been married to the same woman
almost fifty years, has a son
who sells life insurance,
a daughter in Topeka, three grandkids.

And now I hear it, too.
How his heart that once said... *today*
... *today*... now seems to say
remember me... remember me...

THE WAGES OF MERCY

The medics tell me he's been ten years
in the nursing home, dwindling
the past few weeks, refusing to eat,
asking only for his Winstons
and to be left alone.
Tonight when he spiked a fever,
and quickly became unresponsive,
with no family, no friends
to contact, the nurses asked
he be brought here, to the Emergency Room,
the open hands of strangers.

His color is awful. He's barely breathing.
I wonder for a moment what all
the commotion is about,
nurses frantically starting IVs
and drawing blood and
placing EKG electrodes;
it's only death—
as if we hadn't seen death before.

I shine a penlight into vacant
eyes, touch his heaving chest
and abdomen with the bell
of my stethoscope, listening
to the pneumonia crackle and pop.

The nurses ask what I want to do,
as if we must do something, anything.

I stroke a lock of matted hair
away from the old man's brow,
order a liter of saline and
some oxygen, biding time with comfort
as I sit at his bedside,
rifle through his voluminous chart.

Cardiac monitors beep and whir,
keeping guard with their syncopated melody.

The telephone rings three times, then stops.

LABYRINTHITIS

Five months ago, the telephone
rang: a voice saying his father
was dead—a ruptured aneurysm
early Sunday morning
while he was in the garden
clipping roses.

Now there's a ringing
in his ears, the room spinning
when he turns, and he's beginning
to wonder if he's not becoming
his old man.

He fidgets on the exam table,
kneading palms, as I narrate
the inner ear's anatomy, how rhinovirus
upsets our bearings.

We went boating the week before,
the man says, *and he was fine.*

I silence myself to listen
to whatever he has to say, and imagine
how for five months the words   *father   dead*
must have looped inside him.

How they entered his ears like a pair of ravens
and flapped against his tympana, began
a rippling inside each fluid spiral
and funneled deeper, deeper. No longer as words,
but as shadows of words, a hush
left for him to unravel.

LITANY

—for V. 1982–2000

Voice coarse from weeks of chanting,
he tells me one hundred nights have passed
since his son was killed, time now for his soul
to emerge from the bardo,
enter a new life. But he fears his grief
like an upturned root
will cause his wandering son to stumble,
make him a shadow forever.

His boy would have been eighteen, reborn
today as a man. Instead his father is a man
with only ghosts for sons.
Furrowed with the telling, his litany
begins anew:

If only I'd given him the five dollars
If only I'd asked him to stay, make his grandmother another cup of tea

He was a strong boy,
as different from his parents as bread from rice.
Bored with high school's jocks and hall monitors,
he began to roam the projects at night, as if haunted,
as if in search…

If only I'd been less strict
If only we'd returned to Cambodia

Was it the Cambodia of his ancestors, with its vast jungles and wats,
the place his grandmother spoke of only in whispers?
Resting place of three older brothers, barely remembered,
toy soldiers disappeared in Pol Pot's war?

Or was he searching for his true mother—
who nursed him and sang to him long nights in the Thai camps—
not this shell of a woman, insane with grief,
who wanders now from neighbor's house to neighbor's house.

I thought it was a car backfire
a neighbor slamming the door

Perhaps the gangs and cocaine
were a way of belonging.
His first high a glimpse of the bardo's long sleep,
a release from this in-between life.

If only I'd looked out the window
If only I'd gone outside to see

Perhaps his father might have seen the car approach,
heard the door creak open, his son's muffled cry.
Perhaps he might have called to him
before the gunshot opened a hole in his head,
a doorway he could never shut.
Perhaps he might have held him
still alive where he lay, curled like an infant
in a pool of his own blood.

I thought it was a car backfire
If only I'd asked him to stay, make his grandmother another cup of tea

I tell him, "You were a good father,
you did all you could." And I see
how he wants to believe me,
how he wrings his hands and bites his fists,
brown eyes becoming two pools.

He asks me to go with him to the pagoda,
help chant his son toward a happy life.
Amid dizzying incense and ringing bells

I join him singing the *phowa*,
and dwell for a moment in that radiant doorway
where birth becomes death
and death becomes birth:
one hand washing the other.

WHAT IS LOST

…everywhere and always
go after that which is lost.

> —Carolyn Forché, "Ourselves or Nothing"

When she came across the border
she had no shoes—only one black
Cambodian skirt, a thin blouse, the long
scarf they use for everything: sleeping,
bathing, carrying food, wrapping
the bodies of the dead.

She no longer wants to say
what happened to her husband and brothers,
afraid if words bring them back,
along will come the soldiers.

What do I have, she asks,
to keep the nightmares away?

Next to her guttural vowels
and clipped consonants, my English
strikes a tin note. The interpreter
translates my advice, and I wonder
which sound was *nerve,* which
was *heart,* which *grief.*

I give her another pill to try.
Perhaps with this one
she will sleep well
tonight. A sleep untroubled
by dreams, by memory.

She listens politely, smiles
a thank-you: her only English.

Yet as I watch her leave
I know her cure comes Tuesday afternoons—
when she joins the circle
of other Khmer women to sew.
Punctuating the fabric
with yellow thread, binding her remnants
into a piece that will hold.

A HOLE IN THE WEB

At the present time, smallpox lives officially in only two repositories on the planet… now exotic to the human species… there is not enough vaccine to stop an outbreak.

—Richard Preston, *The Demon in the Freezer*

1

After two days of high fever, dry cough,
a puzzled look appears upon the face.
A rash covers the body all at once,
each shotty pimple dimpled in the center.
If the pustules merge into painful sheets
the victim usually dies, his whole skin
splitting off. In extreme cases the flesh
remains smooth and intact, then darkens
as if charred. Black unclotted blood oozes
from mouth and anus. The few survivors
will report they were acutely alert
and aware—helplessly sunk in a kind
of paralyzed shock, watching their poor life
bleed out amid a sickly odor—skin
giving off as yet unexplained gases—
as armies of the brutal virus disperse
invisible as air to other hosts.

2

No wonder we've wanted for centuries
to rid the planet of it: old friend, un-
invited guest, that grew with us in our
first villages, first farms; ancient Chinese
exposing their children to its weaker
cousin, *variola minor*; English
milkmaids with cowpox-covered hands the source
of the first vaccine. In time, Big Science

would track it down like a fox, scour it
from every village and jungle until
not a trace remained. Put the thing on ice:
not alive, not dead, but held in suspense—
impotent and lethal as a zero.

3

Seven small scabs, frozen in glass vials
in a lab somewhere in America—
peeled with tweezers years ago from the arm
of little Rahima Banu—a three-
year-old Bangladeshi girl who survived
the last case of *variola major*
occurring in the wild—are all that
remain of this once onerous pox. She's
a mother herself now, a grandmother,
marked by pox scars, but alive. Her legacy:
never to see another child blossom?

4

As if trying to free a dog of his mites,
a beach of its sand—the weedy flower
the gardener carves back to its roots may
return in spring, spiraling with vigor.
And one day in New York, a Long Island
taxi driver might open a glass vial
someone's left in his cab, sniff its gray dust.
Two weeks later, a Boston businessman
will come down with a cough, and the next
apocalypse will have begun. Imagine
the ever-expanding whorl of cases,
its familiar pattern unrecognized
until too late, the silent petals
of a poisonous flower opening.

WHAT MATTERS

—for Eric

The nurse drifts in, checks
the level of the morphine drip.
We let our eyes wander from you
to the windowsill of poinsettias
framing the snowbound city below.
From the sink of white porcelain
to the field of white that covers
your body, uncomfortable in our comforting
because there is nothing more
for us to do now but attend.
We close our eyes, listen to you breathe.
Pause when you pause, linger over each
exhalation as if it were your last.
That you circled the world as a merchant
marine, spent seven years in a monastery,
raised show dogs and exotic birds,
no longer seems important.
What matters is now, this moment.
How quiet your room has become,
only the sound of the winter sun
streaming through panes of glass.
We kiss your face, squeeze your hand;
hang on before we let go.

BREATH

—for Mark Catuska

Called late to your bedside,
I feel almost an intruder, but join
the whirl of watchers
gathered by your sinking.

Potted gerberas, ghastly in fluorescent
light, wilt on the tray table. If your mother
were here she'd water them, trace the jagged scars
a car crash carved in your scalp
the summer you turned seventeen.

We almost lost him then.

Suction tubing uncoils from the wall.
A deflated blood pressure cuff
lies abandoned on the linoleum floor.

Remember the Halloween party
you cornered me in the back hall, grinning
with your ghost face,
Who's gonna be your trick tonight?

Did our circle merely grow apart,
or was the vortex of your illness
too suffocating for any of us to hold?

The oxygen mask hisses, your breath
rises and falls, in and out, heave and huff,
an awful rowing.

Your team of midwives, we breathe
with you in transition, grip your hand,
stroke your hair, mop the pearls
from your shining head.

DANS LE PALAIS NOSTALGIQUE

— Teatro Zinzanni, Seattle, New Year's Eve, 1999

This Belgian *Spiegeltent* has survived a century
of silly wars and rock operas, ominous comets
and death camps—her jeweled brocade and red velvet,
oak posts and beveled mirrors, like us, relatively intact.
Perhaps that's why, taken under her wing, we allow ourselves
to float upward to the canopy's narrow peak
where a fiery-haired woman in leopard-skin tights
descends from a spotlit trapeze barely a thread
above tables draped with flowers and white linen.

Was it another lifetime we first gathered for the feast,
clinking flutes of golden champagne in the plush lobby,
waiting our turn to be granted admittance to the tent's
gracious spectacle, long months of renunciation
winning us this one night of indulgence?
An Elvis in white jumpsuit and cape
leads us to our table ringside in the pavilion,
hums a verse from "Love Me Tender,"
as four couples, all of us men, squeeze into a booth for six.

The pale, meticulous maître d', a Ukrainian
Lurch the Butler, inspects our table setting,
miming his dis-humor with a drop of his monocle, carefully
adjusting the silverware's alignment, the angle of B.'s
hastily knotted tie, barely allowing the tips of his gloved fingers
to graze across K.'s unshaven chin before
sauntering away—straight-faced, a shower of confetti
cast over his left shoulder in a flourish.

Amid a parade of jugglers and clowns, the sumptuous courses
appear: a heaping platter of herbed mozzarella,
prosciutto, baked garlic, olives, and fine toasts;

then bowlfuls of creamy butternut squash soup
garnished with sautéed mushrooms, a spritz of red pepper oil
delivered by the ridiculous lovelorn
dishwasher Juliet, who laughing, snaps our picture
while straddling a gentleman's lap at the next table.

We slurp and suck upon wilted spinach salad
topped with poached salmon and apricot,
a main course of chicken parmesan and *fines herbes,*
the waitstaff revealing themselves as part of the show,
dashing about with heaping plates of hot potatoes,
stopping to hoist our bottle of Petite Sirah
high above their white-hatted heads to pour,
joining to croon a fool's version of "Auld Lang Syne."

For tonight, life is an elegant, endless jest:
the stacks of falling dishes are unshattered plastic;
the pickpocket busboy returns with your wallet
as the gendarme's pistol shoots a bouquet.
In a wig and sequined evening gown, the head chef,
winking, inquires if our chicken was "... *tender,*"
and the woman sawed in half
returns to offer us dessert, asking—seriously—
if we'd like to split the check.

And now this: the world-famous chanteuse
pausing at our table with the spotlight upon her.
And J., who once believed he'd never live to see
the new millennium—his wasted body now well
and healthy—gazing into the eyes of the Diva
as she sings "... *haven't we met like this before...,*"
takes his outstretched hand, then slowly wanders on, to vanish
with the gypsy caravan into the tented night,
leaving us ravished, our stomachs and hearts full.

TAKE CARE

Take care, we say to one another,
on parting, as if the cargo
we carried were fragile
or dangerous—chipped
bottle of nitro, crystal
blue robin's egg, last ampule
of the healing serum.

II

CHAMBERED NAUTILUS

At first it seems random, this leaving
one life only to reemerge within another.
Yet looking back over your shoulder
things begin to take shape, a pattern
unfolds, where you've been a procession
of ever-enlarging rooms, a spiral
circling out from its center.
We cannot escape history.
In a moment of contemplation
it's easy to return ourselves
to an earlier self, to recall
at age five the way smoke curled
in the sunroom as you watched
your father crush out his cigarette,
stand, and slowly unhitch his belt.
To remember how it felt
at sixteen to push your face
into a cold cement floor and cry out
with grief and abandon
as a Texas trucker took you from behind;
at twenty-one to say
for the first time to another man
you loved him, only to watch him turn
and walk out the door;
at thirty to bury him
and start all over again.
We construct our lives around us,
four walls, a door, some pictures on the mantel
in a room that seems to remind us of home,
a set of conditions within which
we are satisfied
to exist for a while, bringing in
a few friends for dinner on a summer evening,
saying things we believe will matter,

until one day we sense the walls closing in,
there's no longer enough room,
and we find ourselves breaking away,
setting out in a car, alone with few belongings,
hurtling down the highway
in search of another vacancy.

ECHOLALIA

Perhaps it's language, in the end,
confuses us, confuses him.
Indifferent as a tape recorder, he gives back
only what we've given.
Does that mean his mind is empty
as a canyon, blank as
a canyon wall? Or that he's saving
his own words for other ears?
Strange mirror to ourselves, my nephew:
by seven he can scrawl
the four letters of his name on command,
knows all the colors of M&M's by heart.
Yet our syntax he'll only ape,
his sentences a stringing together of noises
used less for communication than ritual,
more for the pleasure of the sayer.
Where's Daddy? Where's Daddy?
He's gone. He's gone.
Repeated over and over for an hour
until we wonder if he understands
more than we do that his father, gone
two years now, is never coming back.
He cannot tell us exactly how he feels,
yet he alone remains chattering
over the 500-piece Big Ben
we gave him last Christmas,
long after the rest of us can only
cup our hands over our mouths,
having nothing more to say.

THE BOY WHO PLAYED WITH DOLLS

remembers the family photograph
of him in shorts, knees pressed close,
the toes of his sandals touching.
A missing tooth makes an awkward smile
as he gazes into the camera,
wincing as if the flash has wounded him.
The two large dolls are naked,
hair shorn, arms and legs akimbo
as they dangle from his hands.
Even at five years old
he is too tall to hold them
so their feet like his
will touch the ground.
Years later, his mother will say:
You weren't a sissy, you were practicing
to be a doctor.

KAFKA'S GRAVE

Curled on my lap like a cat
my nephew colors airplanes and helicopters,
potent images from the imagined life
of his father, a military man
who disappeared without leaving anything
written, without ever hearing his wife
call out in childbirth, or his
only son mouth the family name.
It's uncanny the resemblance
between this child and myself; a stranger
would think he was mine, yet
I'll surely never be called father
or husband by anyone in this life—
as his grandmother blithely explains:
Your uncle's the artistic type.
Concealed in evening light I carry
my half-asleep nephew up the stairs
to his bed, wondering if I too abandon
a son being who I am, his mother's
bachelor brother, a gay man, a writer.
I bend to kiss the boy's cheek,
then turn out the light.
I will never author a living child.
Nearing forty, possessed at last
of the right to an entire bed,
an entire house, an entire life to myself,
I fill my pen with ink
and wander out to the wooden bench
under the flowering plum to write.
Kafka died childless,
a bachelor surrounded by books
he never saw published; yet even
in the dead of winter his grave's
alive with loving flowers—
as if among the yard of markers
only he had living progeny.

BLACK NARCISSUS

Her arms swimming in the languid
June heat. I'm watching my mother
deadhead spent daffodils—
thinking of the summer my sister
disappeared off the deep end
of the motel pool in Coeur d'Alene.
How a faded tuft of her auburn locks
was all we saw, swirling the surface
as chlorine waves lapped drain screens.

One white hand emerged, opened
like a lily, then vanished, before my mother
lunged for the seaweed tangle of hair,
lifted her child's gasping body
straight up out of the water
to the lull of a cement ledge—
one quick flawless movement—
as if she were weightless.

She didn't know then, that it would be
her *younger* daughter,
the one with black hair and eyes,
asleep poolside in the bassinet,
who three years later would die,
blood and urine laced with a terrible sweetness,
her drowned breath an acetone mist.

Perhaps that's why, each summer, my mother
pulls up all her bulbs, exhumes them
one by one—daffodil, tulip, dahlia,
hyacinth—before the creeping autumn rains
begin, before any of them can be lost.

SUITE FOR A SISTER

1. Sustenance

My sister was very sick.
I wanted to be a good brother,
help my mother carry the chicken soup
and orange juice to her room.

I remember how she opened her eyes
and smiled at me, how she took a sip
of juice and went back to sleep.

The next evening she was dead.

Origin
of my twin
vocations:
poetry and medicine.

One the study of grief,
the other the study
of silence.

2. Madrona

My sister died when she was five.
Sugar diabetes, my mother said.
And I had to pee in a cup

to see if I had it, too.
I didn't and lived.

Later I had an awful cavity.
It kept me up at night.
Too many sweets, my father said,

and took me to the dentist
where the hollowed tooth was filled.

My sister died when she was five.
I went on and lived—

but like this madrona
always bent to the earth,
roots clinging to the cliffside,

half dying, half alive.

3. I Dream My Sister Is Abducted by Aliens

Our family is camping at Larrabee State Park when we wake up to find she
is gone. My father examines the long slit cut cleanly with a laser in the tent
side, gaping open like a fish mouth. They even took her sleeping bag!
At first I am afraid, but it's daytime and the aliens have vanished. My
mother wants to look for her but we have to eat breakfast first and there
is no milk, only little boxes of dry cereal, each one lying on its back with
its front cut open.

4. Suzy Q

After my sister died
our family bought a boat,
named it after her.

Summers we'd go motoring
across the lake's gray eye,
the smell of diesel oil
mixing with the dead
smell of the beach.

I'd sit on a plastic cushion
tying and untying a rope knot,
the *thump, thump* of waves
filling the hollow of my chest.

We still have the photographs:
Father at the wheel staring
straight ahead, Mother
in her sunglasses
trying hard to smile,

all of us children
strapped into life jackets.

5. I Dream My Sister Is Still Alive

and in Fresno, married ten cheerful years to a computer geek she met
in high school. They have three kids, two girls and a boy. She's driving a
minivan and taking them to soccer games. She's shampooing the girls' hair
and gently brushing it dry before bed. She's baking chocolate chip cookies
for their school lunches and checking her blood sugar and injecting herself
with insulin. I feel so glad I could cry. How much she looks like me.

VINCENT

Thanksgiving he'll be there, crumpled
corduroy jacket, red hair slicked over, eyeglasses
jury-rigged with a safety pin: your older brother.
With vigor he'll shake your hand, say he's glad
to see you, though you know your mere presence
brings back the day he returned
from summer fishing in Alaska,
his vision changed, his voice
more buoyant, as if a transfiguration
had occurred out there on the rolling ocean
where he'd survived three months cooped up
like Jonah inside the whale. Seeing you
he'll remember nights he was awake past two
furiously writing letters to senators, mornings
he arose before six to mow the front lawn
again, how he told you he'd seen the devil
riding the 6 Stoneway bus—
indolent beginnings of a mania
that would derail two weeks later
in a stolen car twisted around a telephone pole.
Now pills keep him docile
as a cow; but you know the voices
haven't stopped—he's merely been rendered
immune. Siren cries still lure him
to return to Alaska, where the skies
are blue as sapphire and wild bears
eat from the palm of his hand; where he captains
a mighty fishing boat and a bar full
of lipsticked women adore him. Perhaps
it's their unearthly din he's trying to silence now,
bandaging his ears with headphones,
filling the room with his own voice.

HIKING TO TSAGAGLALAL PETROGLYPH, THINKING OF GUY ANDERSON AT 90

High above the valley, where midday sun makes a kiln
of treeless rimrock, I stand in supplication before her.
Mother of everything, mouth drawn taut by the centuries,
her long-ago composed eyes keep watch as the Columbia
gorges its path to the Pacific. The Yakama say

she remembers when Celilo was the world's center. How the waters
thundered down rocky chutes and ledges, infinite salmon
jumping in the mist. This was before the dams rose
and drowned villages; before railroads and wagon trains;
before death came floating on its dark steamer.

Now the basalt cliffs that frame her solemn face
flake and crumble, giving way as I climb
to bare rolling steppes, the clefted sinews
of the basin's great unfinished canvas. Resting here,
I think of the gentle Northwest painter

at 90, how the angular clutter and affliction of his early work
gave way in his later arrangements to the soft
rounded sumptuousness of male and female nudes
drifting above egg-like spheres, each one tethered
to a wide oceanic void by an umbilical streak of red.

As if time's rolling could make us smooth
and plump as babies again. Our arid fixities
dissolving as our wrinkled eyes and hands surrender,
until all that remains is a wisp of silver in the twilight,
the blank O of a moon rising over water.

WINTERBLOOM

—for Carol

1

The knot in your breast was already
the size of a garlic clove; we stood with you
amid the arboretum's bare trees,
hardly speaking, as if a war
had just been declared.
Then we descended a damp trail
to where a Chinese witch hazel
that day had burst into bloom,
its papery petals capturing the light,
filling the air with a sweet
faintly medicinal fragrance.
We stopped for a photograph,
perhaps the last with your famous red head of hair
intact. How I hated them then,
those beautiful flowers,
blooming when all should be at rest.

2

Two years later, chemo completed
and your amber-red hair
returned, those same flowers seemed a blessing,
a sign of life returning
after the chasm of a long winter.
You said you felt cured
and laughed as we walked
beneath the frosty, sunlit branches.
But you never made it to year three.
And now as I walk the winter garden
thinking of you, your witch hazel
is in bloom again, its red-orange tatter
a shimmering confetti, its citrus-musk
a bitter sweet.

MELANCHOLIA

—Dürer, 1514

All afternoon I worked and reworked my idea:
but nothing would cohere. Mind crowded
with puzzles, I swept the table clear, retreated
to this window seat, this simmering
November sky, thinking how heavily
Dürer's winged angel sits upon her low step,
head in hands, amid a heap of cast-off baubles.

Her shadowy face glowers fiercely,
to where her compass, pen, and ruler
lie abandoned—even as her eyes
peer elsewhere: bright, almost glaring,
as if by a sudden volt of intellect
or will, she has surmounted the clutter
and at this instant arrived cleanly
upon a creation entirely new, and pleasing.

Is it the sphere, freshly rolled from her lap,
perfect and glowing as a pearl? Or does her gaze
focus beyond, where none of us can see,
her mind finally emptied and,
like these bare trees awash in amber,
framing what it cannot contain.

III

WINDOW SEAT

Pillow-propped, secluded by a double layer
of leaded glass, cocooned with my books, I
am inside, watching you
tromp the rain-drenched garden in boots,
clouds of breath rising as you rake
dead leaves into heaps.

Working, you cannot hear
my mind race, cannot hear me struggle
to force an idea beyond the margins
of this page, follow a thought
out to its reasoned end.

Yet when I call your name, you stop,
lean against the rake's upright handle,
remove your red handkerchief, and mop
the beads from your neck. You turn
not to me, but to the white sky:
and for what? Absence of blue?
The failed premise of snow?

LEARNING TO TWO-STEP

I'll always remember how we *promenaded*—
kitchen linoleum to living-room carpet,
across bedroom hardwoods and back again—
the *slow, slow, quick-quick, slow*
of those rented years in two separate
one-bedrooms, four flights up
in the same vine-covered brownstone.
Our *to* and *fro* was a strange dance of intimacy growing:
you in the lead, but forever marching toward me,
as I followed, but forever backed away.

Nights of just the two of us—
and Randy Travis
crooning from the stereo
as I learned to ride your thigh,
gaze into your eyes. I wanted to be
where this was going, to feel us dip and spin
amid the Timberline's strobing parquet,
the blue-jean decussation of our legs
marking time with the black-leather glide
of boots across a salt-grained floor.

But our four left feet never mastered
this simplest of steps, though for weeks we tried:
stubbing toes and stumbling
together in a boisterous heap, each of us
believing we would never be sad
again, never be sad
in this way again.

THE BIRTH OF FLOWERS

Imagine the shock—
amid a vast expanse of conifer
and moss, homely liverwort and ginkgo—
when the first petals appear

supple and pink as unknown human flesh,
pushing aside ancient horsetail and fern,
hue almost electric against
the unending green and brown.

Imagine the first sepals parting
to reveal stamen, pollen-dusted pistil,
the fragrance and honey of sex
both lurid and intoxicating—
the dizzying perfume
of earth become a boudoir.

And then the rapid proliferation
of forms and varieties, teeming meadows
orange and red and purple-throated.
The coming of tubers and bulbs,
seeded and pitted fruits,
hermaphroditic orchids.

Scientists would have us believe
it's all genetics, natural selection, survival
of the fittest—but can't explain
the sudden appearance of flowers.
So fragile and so useless,
of no great purpose, no obvious advantage.

Yet somewhere in the mid-Mesozoic,
post-Jurassic era, as if from the dark
emptiness of a long winter, the first spring
came to the planet, eggshell white
tinged with purple streaks—
and a new world bloomed.

SENSELESS BEAUTY

A breezy updraft whips cirrocumulus
high off Rainier's snowcapped peak—
like sea spray from a wave tip.

First full day of T-shirt and shorts,
wisteria twining the cedar trellis,
the garden rising into the crisp spring air.

What's the point except
                              there is no point?

Our neighbor with throat cancer
hoped the radiation burns would heal
before he starved—and now

I hear his voice singing across the yard.
Fat robins flap and splash in the birdbath.
Stands of poppies open their red hearts.

The sky so damn blue.

SHADOW AND SPIRIT

We were half-undressed in the bedroom when
   the call came: Officer Loveless breaking
the news our car was found near Seward Park,
   crashed, right tire blown, the engine on fire.

Two brothers, juveniles, stole a pair
   of Dodges that night—our '90 Shadow,
a neighbor's '92 Spirit—raced them
   to the back door of a girl they knew.

Apparently, having two boys want her
   was as irresistible as the hip-hop
bouncing from our radio, bass up full blast.
   She chose the Shadow, and got in (what kids

won't do for love...). They cruised up and down
   Lake Washington Boulevard like billionaires,
smoking beanies and weaving through traffic
   until the blue and red of a patrol car

began to flash in the rearview. Both boys
   sped off in opposite directions, paired
police chases ending at the same
   dead-end roundabout outside the park.

Our car high-centered on a grassy rise
   and smashed into a park sign, airbags blown,
starshape in the windshield, blood dripping down
   the boy's face as he hopped out, ran for it.

The girl, uninjured, tried to mix in the crowd—
   while our Shadow smoldered, sparked a small fire—
then feigned amazement when the cops cuffed her,
   saying, "But, I didn't even *know* him!"

How sad, we thought, returning to our bed,
   picturing her left inside the patrol car,
face shadowed by flames—a love-lost child,
   cuffed wrists making a heartshape of her hands.

LOFT BEDROOM, TRANQUILITY COTTAGE, ORCAS ISLAND

We face the open window, let the salt
air from Harney Channel blow
across our naked bodies.
On the shoreline, black water sieves
through beach gravel and bleached driftwood
as we drift in and out of sleep,
life in the city far behind us,
our ears tuned to bat-wing and flittermouse,
an ancient madrona gently creaking
in the late summer night.

Suddenly, the lights of a passing car ferry
flood our room—amid the splendor of sodium beacons,
fluorescent tubes, spotlights and hall lamps,
the decks are empty, all the passenger seats
abandoned. I try to wake you—but the ghost ship
disappears beyond a stand of cedars, its idling turbines
fading quickly into the darkness.

Then the world is deadly calm.
I feel your chest rise and fall, wonder
if I had imagined it—the sudden light,
the vacant ferry awesome as a Rilke angel.
I am ready to let the image go, when
slowly, with a gentle rocking cadence,
the wake begins to wash against the shore.

IN AUGUST, MY SISTER

and her husband bring the new baby.
We ogle her in the shade
while their two boys play
in our garden, chase each other
around rosebushes, hide
behind the staked tomatoes.

That night we make love,
and after, you stand at the open window
watching grapevines filter moonlight,
the pool of our semen, translucent
on my belly, still warm.

In the guest room below,
the baby is crying. I hear
my sister rise, imagine the infant's
mouth rooting for her breast.

You slide into bed beside me,
the welcome coolness of your flesh,
and I wonder how it will be
to lie together in our graves.

Unmultiplied, undivided, our love
that will not condense
into a life.

WAITING FOR SOPHOCLES

Was there hope for peace in talk of war?
Or was it merely a terrorist act,
a ploy to draw me in, to wage
a losing battle on foreign soil.
A streak of summer days without rain.
You asked me if I was happy
and now I wonder what that means,
wonder what it is you want from me
that I'm not giving. I can't stand
this endless questioning in the dark before bed—
as if love were some sort of interrogation,
neither of us willing to betray
anything but mutually assured surrender.
We've been at this war so long I've forgotten
what we're fighting for now besides pride.
The disputed border between us
riddled with triggered mines.
Lying here, the weight of your arm
across my chest is almost unbearable.
Why do affairs merely end, while marriages
must endure until they fail?
We agree to take the boat back to the mainland
in the morning, return to the home front,
cut the vacation short.
It's enough peace for our bodies to slip
together like a pair of matched spoons
as we wait for the amnesia of sleep
to cover us, the first drops
of summer rain to fall in the darkness.
In the morning we make love
without kissing, without saying a word.

PAS DE DEUX

Odd to be scarfing scrambled eggs & toast
for dinner; odder still for you to stop

midsentence, your mouth half-full, half-open,
as if searching for the best next word—

a puzzled look spreading across your face
like a cape-shadow across a stage floor.

What scared me was your silence, wide-eyed
and panicked, your mouth making a mime's O.

You stood from your chair and I shuffled
behind, clumsily wrapped my arms around you,

placed my fist in the pit of your stomach,
locked hand over wrist, and pulled—

our bodies in a bunny hop—
lifting you a little off the floor.

I squeezed and lifted again. And again.
Like a tango's fits and starts: What was I doing wrong?

I began to lead you across the floor
toward the telephone, trying to visualize

911 on the keypad, imagining what I might say
to the operator, my own throat pounding.

Then you bent forward, as if to take a curtain call,
and the morsel popped out like a wad of confetti.

You gasped, coughed a strong, hardy cough,
said, *I'm OK, I'm OK,* your voice rasping, hoarse.

The kitchen lights flickered, the air hummed with nervous electricity
and a crackling sound something like applause.

LOST

An already dog-eared map
torn and flapping between us,

we learn to avoid *corti*—blind alleys—en route
    to the *salizzada*'s wide street with shops,

      that a *sottoportego* disappears *under* a building,
        while a *campo* is an invitation

        to stop at a café table,
    sip a cupful of fresh cappuccino,

    nibble hot basil-and-tomato focaccia,
and recover our bearings.

We notice Venetians are as inventive
    at spelling as they are at food:

    the sign for this square written
        three ways: *San Biagio, San Biasio, San Blasio*—

    each one delicious.
    Farther on, we stand dumb

    as two placards for the way to *San Marco*
point in exactly opposite directions.

Clearly, this maze of crooked cobblestones
    has no firm intention of leading anywhere,

    Venice a labyrinth we'll never solve.
        At the information kiosk, a man sells picture postcards

      of commedia dell'arte characters,
    all dressed in carnival finery.

      Flummoxed by our wayward wayfinding
we choose suitable personae for our day—

the senile Pantalone in his bright red leotard for you,
        the know-it-all Il Dottore, "from Bah-LOAN-yah," for me—

    stow our map in the knapsack,
            and follow our feet. The myriad canals mirror

            and multiply, their jade waters shimmering
    amid stucco and shutters as we cross

    the next footbridge, our masquerade intact,
improvising our lines as we go.

WINTER STRIPPING

After the pear, the grape, the old apple tree,
we turn to the rose, its cathedral of thorns
vaulting over the trellis. With gloved hands
we untie long canes, let them spring free,
creaking in the still air. Then we begin
the cutting of hardwood and hips.

I think of pain, my own and not my own.
The trunk of letters my mother keeps
in her attic. The gardens my father
planted each year and abandoned.
The children they made, not one of us
planned, just something else that happened
and, like the weather, endured.

If we do this to allow more light,
encourage flower and fruit, create
a more pleasing shape, is the same true
of our lives: the revision
we practice when we consider the past?

I stand back to survey our work.
The severed trunks, the bleeding sap.
I think of the lopped arms
of Venus de Milo.
The beauty of what remains.

THE WINEPRESS

In this day of serial monogamy
and microwave cuisine, when baking anything
has become a lost art
and writing letters
is akin to making lace
by hand, our neighbors give us a winepress.

We have a small grape arbor, bursting
with sweet grapes each summer;
and we like wine; so we scour the used
bookstore and sit up late one night
perusing an illustrated manual
as if it were a Kama sutra.

Crushers and carboys, air locks
and siphons, sulfite, a suitable
wine yeast: we'll need a lot more
than desire and a press
to make our first wine happen.

I close the book and turn
to the window, where old canes
are just beginning
their yearly return to life.

We may only get fuel oil
or vinegar. That won't matter.
This need not make sense
to have meaning.

DOUBLE MAGNOLIA

Sprouting up from the crushed
stump of a previous life, this tree
is really two—one slightly fuller,
twins joined at the hip.

According to *Western Garden,* one
should be pared, the other made singular,
yet how were we to choose? Lopper and saw
in hand, we paused—paired

ourselves, and accustomed to the fit.
Rooted, less by love as by a certain
coherence of desires, by what can't be
divided. Now, as spring's first lily crowns

crack the sod and bees hunt fragrance,
purple globes open on each branch tip,
weighting them in unison
with their net of nectar.

APRIL ELMS

Jazzed by April's burgeoning mercury,
the giant elm pair creaks and moans, showers us
with another load of seedpods.

Dime-sized papyrus wings swirl
greenish flecks on the wind,
accumulate faster than we can sweep
back porch and windowsill,
unclot gutter and downspout.

Indoors, we find them strewn
along the back stair, settled in kitchen drawers,
littering the living-room carpet.
Caught in our hair, lodged in coat pockets—
each one another reminder
of nature's abundant
redundance.

Persistent as old pennies,
they cling to the bottoms
of our bare feet,
slip into the bathroom,
wind their way into bedsheets.

And this morning, lover,
I found one
pressed to your thigh.

PEACHES

The sapling in his south yard's infected
with peach leaf curl. We're not
surprised—this being Seattle, land
of soggy springs and May frosts. But our neighbor

doesn't seem to mind, and rather than fuss
with weeks of lime and copper sprays, shrugs
and returns to weeding phlox.
Speaking over the fence, we discover

he lives alone, likes to keep to himself.
That he too is infected, but has been well.
He's off to Florence when the first peaches
appear in June. Tufts of fuzz

swelling into plumps of green-orange
as clematis vines ensnare his house.
Midsummer, the fleshy orbs begin
to sag the young branches, but we never

see our neighbor—only the signs
of his return: the patio
swept clean, Sunday paper taken in,
porch light clicked on.

Seafair weekend, Blue Angels tear
across the August sky. His small tree
shivers with peaches. Ripe, golden,
they bob in the humid air,

as a pile of mail, two weeks untouched,
spills from his box. We wonder
what has happened,
cross the yard and knock

at the back door—the heavy fragrance
of peaches rising from the floorboards
where some fallen ones lie split,
their furry lips dribbling nectar.

Unshaven, yawning, he opens the screen
and we see for the first time how gaunt he has become.
He thanks us for checking—no, there's nothing
we can do. He departs in the morning

for family back east. Next evening
we hop the fence and pick three ripe peaches
from his tree. We sit in lawn chairs and eat them
watching the pink-orange sun go down.

A POT OF RED LENTILS

simmers on the kitchen stove.
All afternoon dense kernels
surrender to the fertile
juices, their tender bellies
swelling with delight.

In the yard we plant
rhubarb, cauliflower, and artichokes,
cupping wet earth over tubers,
our labor the germ
of later sustenance and renewal.

Across the field the sound of a baby crying
as we carry in the last carrots,
whorls of butter lettuce,
a basket of red potatoes.

I want to remember us this way—
late September sun streaming through
the window, bread loaves and golden
bunches of grapes on the table,
spoonfuls of hot soup rising
to our lips, filling us
with what endures.

GIVING WAY

It seems we've been granted
a reprieve: together on the front porch
regarding what remains of a ruby sky,
languorous branches of the willow
swinging low to brush the sidewalk,
a bee climbing the spire of the last
blue delphinium, all the portents and signs telling us
the season has reached its cusp.
Dead lawn crackles beneath our feet.
Cornstalks rustle next to tomato vines heavy with red.
The giant sunflower, its spiral
picked clean, droops at the gate.
I bend to touch the fallen stars
of the angel's trumpet and find
not devastation, but this: dark kernel,
oily and impenetrable as stone.
Is this the purpose of the flower? Of all
that we have made? Ah, September—
ninth month fully gravid before us.

COMING HOME LATE

I latch the garage door, retrieve
the evening paper from the zinnia,
its soggy weight
dismal as wet bread.

The porch bulb is out, the house
dark and empty. Still dressed in my blue suit,
I wander the vegetable garden
by the light of an alley lamp
droning above me like a hive.

Early October, the grape leaves
scrolled and falling. The haggard zucchini
and what's left of the tomato vines
collapsing into gold rust.

I feel sad, but satisfied.
The earth turning away, tipping us
toward the north, toward sleep.

At the back door, despite dwindling
light and the night's cool, the chrysanthemum
is covered with new blossoms, each one
the color of pomegranate.

I push my face into spicy blooms, feel
their icy wetness cover my cheeks,
and remember how as children
we washed our faces with snow.

THE LATE ROSE

As I scrape the early morning sheen
of frost from my windshield, I notice the tea rose,
sheltered under the eaves of the carport,
beginning to send a new shoot skyward,
each five-leafed stem facing
the white wall as if to drink from it
all the sun's reflected light, all the day's warmth.

Will it bloom before the first solid freeze?
Each day I chart its progress. Watch calyx swell
and sepals part, the deep vermilion
erupt from within, until one morning—
a papery, wet blossom wafts its faint perfume.

Mid May, this single bloom would be lost
in a pageant of roses. But now, its perfect
form, etched into the icy November sky,
is a kind of solitary miracle.

I think of July's quick roses, which explode
overnight and by the next morning are finished.
How this one opened so slowly, like a lover
who takes his time, who knows savor
is a greater joy than success.

PUTTING THE GARDEN TO REST

Today you clipped long, thin verticals
from the espaliered pear and apple, laid them straight
in three bundles tied with twine.

I dug the vegetable beds under,
turning the heavy soil until it fell black
and loose from the spading fork.

I love this emptiness.
Bare branches making a net for the wind.
The garden tucked under a cover of straw.

We pull dry logs from the woodpile,
carry them in to the stove.
A finch lights on the fence post,

then disappears into the white sky.

SAYING THE WORLD

If a dream is the answer to a question
we haven't yet learned how to ask—
if only I were... if only I... then what
am I to make of these flickerings?
this fading corridor of light?

Supine on a chaise longue,
I watch starlings strip the fig
next door, our grape's golden clusters
almost within reach, and beyond:
the venerable pear laden with fruit.

What bliss it would be to linger here,
not even thinking of netting strawberries,
or when to pick peaches; of saucing
tomatoes, or if this year
we'll produce a decent wine. Intent
only upon the corn's silk
streaming in the breeze, a honeybee
darting about the pink geranium.

Instead, this declination of light
recalls a morning in April, when I walked
among the new beds with such hope,
eager for the season. And that—a day
in late October, when I gazed into the ever-opening
center of the last golden dahlia,
then climbed the back stair to find you
alone at the kitchen window.

It's as if the mere saying of the words:
Comice... Early Girl... Blue Comet...
had made the garden appear; and now
the not saying—has begun to make it fade.
Stand with me for a while.
Imagine the silver lily returning
before we say goodnight.

ABOUT THE AUTHOR

Peter Pereira is a family physician in Seattle and a founding editor of Floating Bridge Press. He received his MD from the University of Washington in 1987 and completed his residency in Family Medicine at the University of Washington Medical Center in 1990. He currently provides primary care to an urban poor population at High Point Community Clinic, in West Seattle. His poems have appeared or are forthcoming in *the Journal of the American Medical Association, North Dakota Quarterly, Poetry, Poetry East, Seattle Review, The Virginia Quarterly Review,* and *Willow Springs*; and in the anthology *To Come to Light: Perspectives on Chronic Illness in Modern Literature.* He was the winner of a 1997 "Discovery"/ *The Nation* Award, and his first chapbook, *The Lost Twin*, was published by Grey Spider Press in 2000. *Saying the World* won the 2002 Hayden Carruth award from Copper Canyon Press.

The Chinese character for poetry is made up of two parts: "word" and "temple." It also serves as pressmark for Copper Canyon Press.

Founded in 1972, Copper Canyon Press remains dedicated to publishing poetry exclusively, from Nobel laureates to new and emerging authors. The Press thrives with the generous patronage of readers, writers, book-sellers, librarians, teachers, students, and funders—everyone who shares the conviction that poetry invigorates the language and sharpens our appreciation of the world.

PUBLISHERS' CIRCLE

The Allen Foundation for The Arts
Lannan Foundation
National Endowment for the Arts

EDITORS' CIRCLE

The Breneman Jaech Foundation
Cynthia Hartwig and Tom Booster
Emily Warn and Daj Oberg
Washington State Arts Commission

For information and catalogs:
COPPER CANYON PRESS
Post Office Box 271
Port Townsend, Washington 98368
360-385-4925
www.coppercanyonpress.org

This book was designed and typeset by Phil Kovacevich using Quark XPress 4.1 on a Macintosh G4. The text typeface, Minion, is a 1990 Adobe Originals typeface by Robert Slimbach. Minion is inspired by classical, old style typefaces of the late Renaissance, a period of elegant, beautiful, and highly readable type designs. Created primarily for text setting, Minion combines the aesthetic and functional qualities that make text type highly readable with the versatility of digital technology. The headings are set in Trajan, another Adobe Originals typeface designed by Carol Twombly in 1989. Trajan is inspired by classic Roman letterforms, which reached their peak of refinement in the first century A.D. This book was printed by McNaughton & Gunn.